The Missing Amish Girl

Hannah Schrock

1

Table Of Contents

The grey of the afternoon was turning to the dusky low light of early evening. All was quiet in the small community, save for the faint barking of a distant dog.

Martha Lehman frowned as she looked out of the bedroom window, surveying the empty street below. It would be dark in an hour and she had expected her eldest *dochder* to return home some time ago. Martha had sent her on an errand to collect a few items from town; a small order from the Englisch bakery and local grocer. It shouldn't have taken this long.

Rebecca Lehman was eighteen years old and very pretty. She had her *daed's* good looks, the same dark hair and piercing blue eyes; deep and wilful.

Martha had noticed a change in her *dochder* over the last few months and every time she was late she worried. Not that she thought Rebecca shouldn't go out and have fun, it was her *Rumspringa* after all; a time for testing the boundaries, but unfortunately Eli didn't see it that way.

She had married Eli when she was just seventeen years old.

Times had been a little different when she was a teenager. Then, young people had been expected to behave in a certain way, even during their *Rumspringa*, and she had never ventured far from her own community. Her own parents had been pleased when Eli had come to call, parking his buggy in front of the house. It had seemed like the perfect match. She had been flattered by the handsome young man's attention, even though he was somewhat serious and pious for one so young. Martha was plain looking; homely her *mamm* had kindly put it, and many of the prettier young girls in the community had vied for Eli's attention.

Yet, it had been the level-headed and mousey Martha that he had chosen - the only girl that did not try to flirt with him. They had spent their evenings together reading *Gott's* words, and whilst she had sat spellbound listening to his voice, he in turn had admired her simple, steadfast beliefs and lack of wonder for the wider world. Martha would make him an obedient and dutiful *fraa*.

That had been a long time ago and she wondered where the years had gone to. She would have liked to have been more adventurous, like her eldest child, but she had not been brought up that way. Sometimes she felt like screaming, longing to voice the feelings that she had pent up for so long—yet she remained silent. Eli had turned into a very traditional and strict husband and *daed*; controlling his family with no real understanding of his two young *dochder*'s and their own views on the world. Everything was black and white to Eli; even his marriage.

Martha was afraid of him, although she would never admit it. Eli had a temper although he had never shown any violence towards her or the girls. There was a violent undertone to his religious zeal and Martha often wondered what he would do if he was pushed too far. Luckily, that had not happened and she maintained the peace within the household. She had been brought up to believe that her place was beneath her husband, not his equal. Sometimes she felt like breaking away; but where would she go to? All her life she had lived in the same village and she knew her place within the community. She could understand why Rebecca wanted to spread her wings and tread a little in the wider world. Martha didn't blame her *dochder* but hoped that she would tread softly; for all of their sakes.

The evening curfew imposed by Eli was 10 pm. Martha sat sewing, patching one of her old dresses by the lamp light. Eli hated any waste and although money was not an issue, he would not allow her to buy material to make new clothing whilst she could mend and make do. He had sat for the last hour in his high back chair, reading from a small black leather bible. Martha noticed the occasional twitch in his jaw; a sure sign that he was angry.

All was quiet except the ticking of the clock, a present from her own mother when she left home. Her parents had a happy marriage, it still was, and the thought almost made her cry.

As the clock hands moved around to 10 pm, Eli Lehman stood up and cleared his throat. Martha put down her sewing and looked up at him nervously.

"I'm going out to look for Rebecca; she should have been home by now"

Martha knew her *dochder* traveled outside of the community, knew that she had *Englisch* friends. She had seen a pair of jeans and strappy top hidden away in her wardrobe but had said nothing. Besides, Eli would never have understood, even if she had.

"It's only just turned ten, Eli, I'm sure she will be home soon. Just wait a while longer, eh?"

Martha was worried that one day he would find her with an *Englisch* boy and lose his temper. If that happened, he would forbid Rebecca to leave the house, or worse, and who knows where that could lead too? A too tight leash was always in danger of snapping!

"Sarah's home, she knows the rules and so should Rebecca. Children should obey their *daed* in all things. How can they obey *Gott's* will if they cannot even obey their own *daed*?"

Eli clenched his jaw as he strode over to the window and looked outside.

"Where is Sarah, doesn't she know where her *schweschder* is?"

Sarah was only a year younger than her sibling, but the two girls were like chalk and cheese and did not get on. Unlike Rebecca, Sarah took after her *mamm* for looks and felt ugly and plain at the side of her beautiful *schweschder*. It had always been a bone of contention between them. Sarah felt that she was second best, that the beautiful Rebecca was the favorite. Even Mark, the boy she had a crush on, only had eyes for Rebecca.

"She's in bed already. She didn't feel well when she arrived home this afternoon and went straight upstairs, and I don't want to wake her."

Eli didn't respond but carried on looking out of the window.

"I'm sure she will be back soon, Eli. It's still early."

It was the wrong thing to say. Eli turned towards her with eyes blazing, his face white.

"Rebecca knows that she must be in the house by 10 pm. She would not deliberately disobey me. There must be something wrong."

He started towards the door, picking up his coat from the chair.

"Eli…?"

Martha stood still, wanting to calm her husband, but it was too late and the door slammed shut behind him.

There would be no peace in the house until he found her.

The sound of the door opening awoke Martha; she had been dozing in the chair and shivered slightly. The room was cold and dark and the cold wind whipped in from behind the open door. The meagre fire in the wood burner had long since been reduced to a pale ash and she rubbed at her arms in an attempt to warm them. Eli looked tired, his face pale in the darkness. He was alone.

Martha glanced at the clock; it was 11:30 pm.

Her heart missed a beat as she stood to greet her husband.

"Well?"

Eli shook his head and looked at the floor.

"I have looked everywhere. I have called at all of our neighbors; her friends - anyone who might know where she is. Nothing. A few of the men helped me to search around the area but we could not find her."

Martha could feel a tightness start to form in her chest.

"We should call the Police!"

His eyes still did not meet hers.

"I have already done that. She is eighteen years old. They said that many young people go missing for a few hours. They told me not to worry…"

"Well then..." Martha tried to smile, to lighten the mood, even if only to convince herself.

Eli approached his *fraa*, hands clenched in front of him.

"I told them not my Rebecca; maybe some *Englischer mann's dochder*, but not mine. She would never disobey her *daed*. If it was Sarah perhaps, but not Rebecca."

Martha remained silent. There was a lot she could tell him about his "perfect" *dochder*, that she was just a young girl and needed to find her own path, but he would not understand. There was no point trying to explain; besides he would never listen.

"I will stay awake in case she returns. You go to bed, Martha. There is nothing you can do."

Nothing **she** *could do!* Martha bristled inside. Rebecca was her *dochder* too, but Eli had to be in control.

"What happens if she doesn't come home?"

"Then I go back to the Police and we search again!"

Martha woke suddenly from a fitful sleep, blinking towards the early morning sun. She could sense that it was still early; the bedroom tinged with the soft yellow light of a new dawn. The space in the bed beside her was empty, the sheets smooth and unruffled. It was obvious that Eli had been downstairs all night. Then she remembered her missing *dochder*, the sudden remembrance causing an ache within her breast. If Eli was still downstairs, then Rebecca was still missing.

Closing her eyes, she offered a prayer to *Gott*.

The room downstairs was empty and cold. The stove remained unlit and the place cheerless.

Opening the curtains wide, Martha let the light fall into the kitchen. She had to keep herself busy. Rebecca would return, she was certain of that and the poor girl would be cold and hungry. Lighting the stove, she allowed herself to be cheered by the flickering flame, the small fire bringing her the warmth of hope. No news was good news; surely?

There was a heavy thud at the door and Eli's bulky frame stood in the doorway. His face was lined and grave and it was obvious that he hadn't slept.

He looked across the room blindly, and she wondered if he had noticed her.

"I'll make you some breakfast?" Hesitating, she wavered over the stove, afraid of voicing the question that was on her lips; the pain in her heart making her afraid.

Eli stood in silence and she wondered if he had heard her.

"I'll make some coffee?"

Crossing the room, he picked up a rucksack that was lying under the window.

"There's no time, besides I have eaten with Joseph Schroder this morning."

Martha felt her heart harden towards her husband; trouble should unite them, not tear them wider apart. She longed to cry and open up her heart to her husband but instead she remained tight-lipped.

The silences within their marriage had never been the comfortable spaces of easy companionship. She had crawled through the last twenty years on eggshells, and now it was too late to change.

As he headed back towards the door, she could no longer keep quiet.

"What is happening, Eli; where is Rebecca?"

He spoke without turning. "I've contacted the Police and they will be arriving shortly. The men of the community are going to help look for her."

"What about me, Eli; what can I do?"

Hesitating, he leaned into the door frame for a moment, as if for support. "Stay here, in case she returns. "His voice waivered as he spoke, then quickly, without another word he slammed the door and was gone.

"What's happening, *Mamm*?"

Martha turned to see her youngest *dochder* looking pale and gaunt, standing behind her at the bottom of the stairs.

Another pain ran across her heart.

Sarah sat with red-rimmed eyes at the table. She too looked like she hadn't slept a wink and Martha wondered how much her *dochder* already knew. Bringing over the coffee, she set the cups down gently upon the table.

"Rebecca didn't come home last night, your *dadd* and some of the other men are looking for her. He's called the Police."

Sarah's dark eyes brimmed with tears as the drops slowly trickled down her face. Martha could feel her pain—the two girls didn't usually get on, but it was obvious that the news had hit her hard.

Sarah's hand trembled as she picked up the cup of hot coffee and Martha frowned.

"Did you know where Rebecca was yesterday?"

Sarah looked into her cup; a sudden interest in the dark brown liquid.

"I thought she was at Katie's, that's where she usually goes to."

Martha liked Katie Zook; she was a sensible girl and had hoped that the girl would be a guiding influence on Rebecca.

"Your *dadd's* asked around all of her friends, but no one has seen her."

"What about Mark?"

Sarah blushed as she spoke his name. The young carpenter was three years older than Sarah and she had a crush on him, even though he only had eyes for the beautiful Rebecca.

"I don't think she hangs around much with Mark. I wish she would, he is a nice boy but she is determined that she isn't interested in him, he would make her a good husband."

Sarah bristled at her words, everything was about Sarah, and no one seemed to care for her feelings.

They sat for a while in another uncomfortable silence. The house was full of them and Martha thought that some days she could scream into the void—but she kept her own counsel. It wouldn't do to make a fuss; she knew her place.

The door swung wide open and Martha looked up to see a young woman standing in the doorway with Eli standing just a little behind her. There was something in her manner that immediately made Martha stand; her hand fluttering to her heart.

"What's wrong?"

"I think you had better sit down, Mrs. Lehman".

Dana Richards was a young and ambitious detective inspector. Police work was her life and she had no time for family life or even a close relationship; she was married to her own career. Good at her job, she was ambitious, some of her colleagues thought her ruthless and perhaps even a little cold.

She hated this part of the job, the distraught families and the tears. She was a detective, not a social worker, but she sat and accepted the coffee from Eli as she watched Martha slowly break down in front of her.

Rebecca Lehman had been discovered in the woods, or at least her body had. The once beautiful face had been covered in blood and there were traumatic injuries to the head from the blow of a heavy object. That was about as much as they knew. Dana was already thinking of the possible murder weapons, listing them in her head whilst Martha Lehman wept for her *dochder*.

If only she hadn't sent Rebecca into town, perhaps she would still be alive, sitting drinking coffee with them now?

Unable to watch her own *mamm's* grief, Sarah rose from the table and walked across to the window and stood silently, staring into the deserted street.

Eli stood at a distance from the table; he could not cry—even for his own *dochder,* but his jaw was set and his face drained. The last piece of hope had disappeared from his heart at the sight of his beloved *dochder* lying in a pool of blood. He had always followed the word of *Gott*, the bible was almost engraved upon his heart; yet at that moment he could not turn the other cheek. His hands clenched together in anger; the fierce inward rage that he had channeled for so long into religious zeal was now breaking to the surface in its purest form. Martha could see the violence in his eyes and she wondered how on earth he was going to make his peace with *Gott*.

It was true, something inside Eli Lehman had snapped; his soul was lost in the wilderness and he wondered why *Gott* had deserted him. Why such pain should be delivered into his life—a life devoted to serving the Almighty?

Dana Richards put down her cup with a clatter that broke the silence of the room. She had been watching Eli Lehman closely as he brooded in the corner of the room and there was something about him, something almost animal like that she did not feel comfortable with. To be honest, she had never believed in God, her world was sterile and factual and there was no room for the spiritual or the make-believe. Besides, she had seen too much horror to ever accept that there could be a creator, a loving Father, a master plan for this crazy earth. However, the Amish had always lived peaceably and even she had to hold up her hand to admit that they had something that was missing from a lot of places, a sense of community and a sense of belonging. Something she had never known.

Eli, however, gave off a different vibe; she too could sense the violent undertones. She had made a mental note of the lack of interaction between man and wife—this couple had issues. Even the *dochder* was strange, wide-eyed and pale-faced and yet unable to cry.

"I'll need statements from all of you, your whereabouts yesterday and this morning. Until we get the post mortem, we won't know the time of death so we will need to establish all of your movements during the last thirty-six hours."

Sarah made a move towards the door leading to the stairs.

"*All* of you, that is."

Eli shifted uneasily at the back of the room, his voice eerily calm.

"Surely you don't suspect her own *familye* of such a despicable act."

Dana Richards sighed as she looked across at the Lehman family.

"At this stage, I suspect everyone."

Martha took her statement first.

She had been home all day, alone—much the same as usual. The two girls had been out during the afternoon; Sarah had a part-time job in the local café, and Rebecca, well, she had thought her eldest *dochder* had been at her friend Katie's but it seemed she had lied about that. The tears fell again as she remembered her sweet *dochder*, it was all too hard to take in.

Next up was Eli. He had been working in the fields, overseeing some planting on the farm. He had been out all day until the evening when he had returned home to discover that Rebecca was missing.

"And what about last night Mr. Lehman, and early this morning?"

The detective inspector's questions were cold and without emotion.

Eli bit into his cheek in an attempt to control his temper; the blood rushing to his brain and clouding his reasoning.

"I was here, where do you think I was? I sat up all night waiting for Rebecca."

"And this morning?"

"As soon as it was light, I set out to speak to the elders of the village to see what could be done—Martha can vouch for that—

can't you?"

His red eyes pierced the space between them and Martha shivered. She had assumed that Eli had been in the kitchen all night, but she could not be certain; everything was confusing. It seemed that she suddenly knew nothing at all.

Nodding her head, she confirmed her husband's statement.

"That's right."

Dana paused, there was something in Martha Lehman's voice that did not convince her, but she would leave it for now. This was only the start of the investigation.

"And finally, Sarah?"

The girl had been watching the proceedings from some distance, and as she approached the table, she looked terrified.

Dana sympathized with the girl, the tension in the room was almost unbearable and she felt sorry for the plain girl in the simple Amish dress. Even in her bloody death, Rebecca had been beautiful, unlike the mousey younger *schweschder*. It couldn't have been easy living in her shadow.

Sarah slowly explained that she had been working at the cafe all afternoon and on returning home had gone straight to her bed having felt unwell.

"That's right, I can vouch for Sarah," Martha interrupted, more certain in her *dochder*'s movements than her husband's.

When the statements had been signed, Dana scraped back her chair and stood to leave.

"Now, I must go and make inquiries in the rest of the community. I have Katie Zook next on my list—I believe she was your *dochder*'s friend?"

For the next few hours, Martha sat alone at the table. Grief made her incapable of any movement and she sat with her eyes fixed towards the window, as if willing Rebecca to return.

Eli had left the house soon after Dana Richards. He could not bear to wait around indoors all day and he had closed the door in silence. Sarah had returned to her room and her own thoughts.

Martha thought of Rebecca when she was a *boppli*. She had been proud of her beautiful first born; even Eli had been proud of his own likeness, the resemblance so strong—even at such an early age. That had been their happiest time together, when she and Eli had been closest. Rebecca had brought them together if only for a brief spell. Eli had been at his most loving towards her, grateful to his *fraa* for bearing him such a bonny *boppli*—a testament to *Gott's* will and grace.

And now, all she could feel was numbness in her heart and a wondering at how she had failed her *dochder*.

A light knock at the door brought her back to the present. Martha didn't feel in the mood for visitors, but, then again, it might be the Police with news.

Slowly, she made her way to the door.

Sadie Zook stood outside, the same grief that Martha felt mirrored in her face. She was the mother of Katie Zook—Rebecca's best friend who had become a confidant and friend to the girl over the years.

"I'm so sorry, Martha."

Martha did not know Sadie well. Eli thought her place was in the home and she rarely had time for friendships. However, Martha knew that Sadie had been kind to her *dochder* over the years and welcomed her in. Maybe she could shed some light onto what had happened, or why?

On auto-pilot, Martha started to make the coffee whilst Sadie sat, trying to find the right words. If it had been her own *dochder* dead in the woods, she would have been inconsolable. The thought was almost too much to bear.

Sadie had liked Rebecca; she had seen a younger version of herself in the sparky teenager. She had felt sorry for the girl too. Over the years, Rebecca had confided in her, told her all about her *dadd* and his control over the *familye*, his temper if they disagreed with him or even dare voice their own opinions. Rebecca had been afraid of Eli; that was certain.

Martha Lehman had the look of the downtrodden about her too; a woman who suffered in silence, the same look of fear in her eyes, like a wounded animal.

"That Police detective called at our house earlier, she wanted to speak to Katie—get some more information on Rebecca."

Martha looked up from pouring out the coffee.

"I don't think she has had much luck. The community is grief stricken and many people are reluctant to speak to the Police. That detective inspector is only doing her job, but I think a lot of people are afraid to speak too much—not that anyone seems to know anything as far as I can tell."

"Oh?"

Sadie stirred her coffee thoughtfully.

"I thought I might ask around, it's the least I can do. Maybe people will be more willing to talk to one of their own, rather than a Police officer? I think she unnerved them. There might be something, however small, that leads us to the person responsible for this terrible thing."

Both women were in tears, and they hugged each other tightly for support. By the time Sadie left, they were good friends, brought together by tragedy.

"I'll let you know how I get on."

As she approached home, Sadie Zook could see the pale face of her *dochder* watching out for her through the bedroom window. Her heart ached to see the young girl so distressed. It had been harrowing to watch the Police detective question her, but now she felt she had to do the same.

Katie was lying back in the bed by the time Sadie had taken off her coat and entered the bedroom. Sitting on the edge of the bed, she smoothed back her *dochder*'s hair from her tear-stained face.

"I've just been to see Martha Lehman."

The girl raised her eyes quizzically.

"No news yet, I'm afraid."

Katie buried her face into the pillow, small muffled sobs escaping from beneath. The poor thing was worn out with crying and Sadie stroked her long hair, waiting for her grief to subside.

Eventually, she rolled over to face her *mamm*.

"Who could have done such a thing? I can't believe anyone would want to kill Rebecca."

Sadie was so glad she could talk openly with her own *dochder*.

"I don't know, my darling. Is there anyone that she was upset with, that she may have fallen out with recently?"

Closing her eyes for a moment, Katie steadied her breathing.

"I think Rebecca had some *Englisch* friend's *mamm*. I think she might have been with them yesterday. They used to hang out at the cinema in town for the late Thursday showing."

"Do you know these girls?" Sadie asked cautiously, wanting her *dochder* to speak freely.

"No, *Mamm*, but I saw them all a few weeks ago when I was shopping in town. They were hanging around by the mall and Rebecca was smoking. She didn't see me and I didn't say anything about it. She had been acting a bit weird lately, and didn't want to hang out with me so much."

It was over a month ago since Sadie had seen Rebecca. She hadn't thought much about it until now. At the time, she had noticed a silver bracelet on her arm, just visible beneath her sleeve. She was going to mention it, but then thought better of it. It had seemed harmless enough; she was in her *Rumspringa* after all. Maybe it had been a sign of something obvious that she had missed?

"Did Rebecca have an *Englisch* boyfriend?"

"Oh, *Mamm*, I don't know. She never said, but I guessed that something was different. I wish I had asked her. I wish I had been a better friend."

Katie sobbed gently in her *mamm's* arms until she was quite exhausted and Sadie laid her gently back on the bed to get some sleep.

Sadie lay awake in bed all night wondering the best course of action to take. She had managed to speak to many families in the village earlier that day, and while they had spoken freely to her, they had little to tell. No one really remembered seeing Rebecca that day, someone thought that they had seen her walking home, carrying Martha's wicker basket. But it wasn't an unusual sight and perhaps it had been another day?

It was at times like these that Sadie felt her faith in *Gott* truly tested. She had suffered when her husband died of cancer several years ago. He had suffered and it had been a blessing when he finally rested. It had been hard on all of them, but this senseless murder of a beautiful young woman was hard to reconcile. Reaching for the bible at the side of her bed, Sadie opened the pages looking for some hope within the scriptures.

The words she read were all about forgiveness, although she could not feel it in her heart.

Turning the pages, she stopped at Matthew 5:21.

"You have heard that it was said to those of old, 'You shall not murder; and whoever murders will be liable to judgment.' But I say to you that everyone who is angry with his brother will be liable to judgment; whoever insults his brother will be liable to the council... Come to terms quickly with your accuser while you are going with him to court, lest your accuser hand you over to the judge, and the judge to the guard, and you be put in prison..."

Sadie felt as guilty of the murder as if she had struck the blow to Rebecca's head herself. Had she let the girl down in some way, had they all let her down? In her heart she felt both the accused and the accuser. The only way left to help Rebecca now was to find her killer; maybe then she would find peace?

The following day Sadie was pleased to see Katie appear at the breakfast table. The poor girl had managed to have some sleep, at last exhausted by her grief. The kitchen was warm and smelled of fresh baking. Sadie had risen early and baked a fruit cake to take to the Lehman's; the two would pay the *familye* a visit to show their respects and maybe find out a little bit more about

Rebecca.

Eli opened the door. He looked older and his face was grey. He spoke little but nodded to them in acknowledgment and opened the door wider to let them in. He would have preferred no visitors but he maintained a facade of good manners and did not want to be seen to go against Amish tradition—however difficult that was.

Martha sat at the table, her head resting on her hands and Sadie wondered if she had been sitting there since yesterday.

The room was cheerless and cold, even with the stove lit; the chill was in their hearts and not in the air. Sadie placed the cake on the empty table and it immediately looked out of place; frivolous for the occasion.

"*Denke,* Sadie."

Martha rose automatically to make the coffee, almost robotic in her actions.

"How is Sarah?"

It was a ridiculous question and it hung heavily in the silence.

"She's still in bed. We thought it best to let her sleep. I heard her crying throughout the night. It has hit her hard, like us all."

Sadie stirred the coffee as Martha sat across from her. Eli remained by the window staring out into the world.

It wasn't a good time to start asking questions, but then there never would be a good time and Sadie hesitated, thinking through her words cautiously.

Setting her cup down carefully into its saucer, she coughed to clear her throat.

"I've been talking to Katie and she thinks that Rebecca might have started hanging around with new friends in town."

The young girl nodded in acknowledgment. Sadie waited for a reaction but none came.

"Katie thinks that Rebecca's new friends were *Englisch*."

Martha looked towards the window at her husband but his back remained turned to them.

"Katie wondered if she had an *Englisch* boyfriend."

Eli turned at her words, his eyes blazing and face twisted in anger.

"How dare you mention such a thing in my house? Rebecca would never do such a thing."

Storming over to the table, he laid his hands on the table, fists clenched to steady him.

"My girl was a good girl. She respected her *daed* and *Gott* and would never have gone against my wishes, unlike some of the young girls in this community."

Katie could feel his eyes bore into her and she looked away.

Placing a hand upon his arm, Martha tried to calm her husband but he shrugged her away.

"Eli, I'm sorry. I didn't mean to upset you. It's just that I think we need to understand what happened. For Rebecca's sake..."

Crossing the room, Eli opened the door.

"I think you had both better leave."

"But Eli..."

Sadie could see the anger simmering deep within in his eyes; it was no use; they would have to leave. Katie looked pale and afraid—no wonder Rebecca had been frightened of her *daed*'s temper.

Exchanging their brief goodbyes with Martha, the two headed quickly out of the door and along the road towards their own *haus*.

"Wait,"

Sadie looked around to see Martha running towards them.

"Sadie, Katie, I'm so sorry. Eli is fraught with grief and he is not himself. Please, can you forgive us?"

Both women collapsed into tears as they stood in the middle of the road and hugged each other. There was no need for forgiveness.

"There is something..." Martha looked around before speaking and lowered her voice.

"I found some *Englisch* clothes in Rebecca's wardrobe—short, skirts, and strappy tops. I haven't told anyone but you. I daren't tell Eli; who knows what his reaction might be?"

"And what about the Police; have you told them this?"

Martha looked troubled. "I didn't mention it. I was afraid that the information would leak out and Rebecca's memory would be sullied. In any case, if I did then Eli would definitely find out. Do you think I did the right thing?"

Sadie smiled and hugged her friend sympathetically. "Don't worry Martha; let's keep it between ourselves for now. Leave it with me and I will see what I can find out."

As Martha walked away, Sadie reached out to hold her *dochder*'s hand. The last twenty-four hours had been a terrible experience and Katie looked tired.

"Are you OK, honey?"

The girl nodded. "I feel sorry for Mrs. Lehman with a husband like that. No wonder Rebecca was afraid of him."

"Well, he's certainly got a temper; I don't know how she can stand it."

Katie squeezed at her *mamm's* hand.

"*Mamm*, Rebecca was scared of her *daed,* I mean really scared. She was convinced that he used to follow her to our *haus*, checking that she wasn't meeting a boy. I don't know what he would have done if he did find out that she was seeing someone, especially an *Englischer*!"

Sadie looked thoughtful for a moment. Her *dochder* had taken the words right out of her mouth.

Once they were back in the house, Sadie started to make a plan. The following day was Thursday, the day that Rebecca usually went to the cinema with her *Englisch* friends. She would check it out—it was her only lead.

Sadie often went into town shopping during the day. There were usually several of the Amish community out and about and the town's people had got used to their simple dress and different customs. All of the shopkeepers knew her and she didn't usually give it a second thought.

At night time, it was completely different and Sadie felt awkward as she stood watching and waiting outside the cinema complex.

Gangs of young people walked past her and she could hear them giggling, high on life if not on other substances. They were probably not even laughing at her but she remembered a time when she was nine or ten years old, waiting outside a shop for her *mamm*. A crowd of *Englisch* girls had gathered round her and teased her—she had never forgotten it and the same feeling of being an outsider suddenly came back to her. It was ridiculous; she was a grown woman—besides she was doing this for Rebecca.

Perhaps it was a ridiculous notion—she didn't even know who she was looking for. As her heart began to sink, four girls walked around the corner. They looked about the same age as Rebecca and one girl was crying as the others seemed to be comforting her. One of them noticed Sadie and whispered to the others and they all looked across towards her.

It was them, it had to be! Sadie felt her heart quicken as she walked over the road towards them.

"Excuse me."

The girls looked up—eyes wide at the Amish woman stood before them.

"Did any of you know Rebecca Lehman?"

It was obvious from their faces that these were the *Englisch* friends that Katie had seen Rebecca hanging out with.

"I'm sorry. I didn't mean to startle you. I was a friend of Rebecca's too, and I wonder if we could all have a chat?"

The electric light inside the small cafe was bright and gleamed off the shiny plastic surfaces. The place was full of young people huddled together; sharing a coffee or a coke and a plate of fries.

Sadie ordered the coffee and the girls found a table towards the back of the room where they could talk with more privacy. The warmth and the light seemed to relax them, this was their territory and they felt comfortable. They seemed like decent girls and all were stunned by the news of their friend.

"Have they caught the man who murdered her yet?" The pale girl who had been crying seemed to have been closest to Rebecca.

Sadie shook her head. "Not yet, the Police don't seem to be any closer with their inquiries. I wondered if any of you girls might know anything?"

One by one the girls looked at each other, unsure what to say.

A pretty girl called Tina with dark curly hair spooned three lumps of sugar into her coffee.

"We used to see her about twice a week; she couldn't come out more regularly because of her Dad." Tina stopped abruptly, aware that she had probably said too much.

"It's OK. Go on," urged Sadie. "I know the family; my *dochder* was Rebecca's friend."

"Well, it's just that she seemed scared of him; or rather scared of what he would do if he ever caught her. She had to sneak out her clothes in a bag. She hated wearing those awful plain dresses and hats. They are so old-fashioned and frumpy."

One of the girls kicked Tina under the table and she blushed, realizing that Sadie was wearing the same type of clothes.

"Oh God, I'm so sorry. No offense, but Rebecca liked to wear the latest fashions, you know?"

Sadie smiled back. "It's OK, I sometimes feel like buying a pair of jeans myself, but I could never walk in high heels," she joked.

The girls laughed and any remaining tension was broken. Sadie could see why Rebecca would have liked their friendship. They were good girls at heart—she had been young once, too.

Sally, the girl who had been crying earlier, leaned forward across the table so she didn't have to speak loudly.

"Rebecca told me that she wanted to leave the Amish community. That she had enough of her controlling Dad and she needed her own life. I think she would have done it too but she was worried about her Mom, worried what her Dad might do if she left. She said he had a terrible temper."

Sadie could feel her chest tighten a little; she was worried about Martha too.

"Rebecca had a younger sister named Sarah; I suppose she was worried about her too?"

Tina shrugged. "I doubt it. I don't think that there was any love lost between those two. Besides, Becky was always talking about this Amish lad who hung around. She liked him but only as a friend; apparently he was mad about her, though. Her kid sister had this crush on him, but he only had eyes for Becky. She kind of hoped that once she had left home the two of them would get together."

Rebecca had often talked about Mark Yoder. He was a nice boy and a gifted carpenter, but she just wasn't interested.

"Did Rebecca have a boyfriend?"

She had hoped the question sounded innocent, but the girls were suddenly wary and glanced at each other around the table. In the end, it was Sally who spoke. "Sometimes we hang around with these guys. There were a few parties and Rebecca came along when she could—although she could never stay out late, she always had to be home by ten. Still, she always managed to have a good time though, a few drinks and a couple of cigarettes, but not too many or else her Dad would find out. She always used to chew a lot of gum to get rid of the taste of alcohol and tobacco and always changed her clothes. There was one lad, Jon, that she was especially friendly with."

Sadie tried to picture Eli's response to the news. It wasn't difficult to imagine his reaction.

The next morning Sadie had a clear plan of action. Sally had told her all about Jon—a mechanic with his own garage just a little out of town. The weather was fine and the place was only a couple of miles walk, besides, the fresh air would help clear her mind. All of the evidence so far seemed to be pointing in one direction, but she couldn't be certain and had to find out more.

Rounding the bend, just on the approach to the garage, Sadie stopped in her tracks. Outside the garage was parked a buggy, obviously of Amish origin. Her heart beat quickly within her chest. What if someone saw her and what if that someone was the murderer? They would know why she was wandering around—there was nothing else in this neck of the woods and she had no other reason for being here.

Rebecca's face flashed through her mind. She had to carry on for the girl's sake.

Walking silently towards the open door, she could hear raised voices from within. Taking a deep breath, she crossed towards the doorway and with her back flush to the garage wall, she peered carefully inside.

At the back of the garage, she could see two men arguing. One man was dressed in overalls and was holding a large spanner—she guessed that was Jon. The other man had his back to her and it took her a moment to realize who it was. He was obviously angry about something and was waving his hands around widely in the air. As he moved his head to the side she recognised him at once. It was Mark Yoder!

Turning away from the doorway, she listened carefully. Mark was shouting, seemingly blaming the young mechanic for Rebecca's death. "If she had been with me, or any other Amish boy, she would still be alive. I would have looked after her. I loved her."

Sadie could hear the pain in his voice.

"Stop shouting at me," Jon sounded firm yet gentle; aware of the other man's grief.

"I loved her too, you know. I had nothing to do with her murder. I could kill whoever has done this."

Mark scoffed "You *Englisch* are only ever after one thing."

Sadie could hear the chink of metal against metal and guessed that Jon had put down the spanner.

"I really cared for Rebecca—OK? She was a beautiful girl, and, of course, I wanted to sleep with her. Who wouldn't? But she kept me at a distance and I respected that. It was too much of an Amish hangover; I suppose? I didn't pressure her. I didn't want to push her into anything she wasn't sure about."

Crossing back over the road, Sadie headed for home; she had heard enough. Until she had more information, there was no point in confronting anyone. Besides, it could be dangerous.

Now she was more confused than ever.

Katie was waiting back at home for her *mamm*. The young girl was worried and had been watching eagerly at the window for her return.

"Well?"

Bringing over a cup of coffee, Katie sat patiently waiting to hear Sadie's news.

"It seems that Rebecca had a boyfriend of sorts. One of her *Englisch* friends told me. I saw him today—he works at the garage just outside of town."

Katie nodded; she had passed it once or twice on trips to see her cousin.

"Well?" Katie was impatient to hear more.

"Well, I walked up to the garage this morning, but guess who was there before me?"

The girl shook her head "I have no idea, *Mamm*"

"Mark Yoder!"

It wasn't a complete shock; Katie liked Mark and knew how keen he was on Rebecca.

"And what happened?"

"Nothing really. Mark was shouting at Jon, blaming him for Rebecca's murder."

Katie's eyes widened.

"Not a real accusation, just that if Rebecca had been his girlfriend, then he would have kept her safe."

"What did the other boy say?"

Sadie sighed. "Well, I sort of felt sorry for him. He said that he loved Rebecca."

"And then what happened?"

Her *mamm* shrugged. "Nothing. They seemed too wound up and I figured that if I had started asking questions, it would have only made things worse."

Reaching across the table, Katie hugged her *mamm.*

"It's too dangerous, you have to stop this. Either one of them could have murdered Rebecca. What if they had seen you?"

Frowning, Sadie ruffled her *dochder's* hair. "I suppose both had a motive. Jon was saying that he hadn't pressured Rebecca into taking their relationship further, and that although he wanted to, Rebecca wasn't so sure. Maybe she had rejected him and he had got angry? And what about Mark? He clearly knew that Rebecca was seeing Jon, otherwise he wouldn't have been at the garage this morning, accusing him."

"And both would have access to a suitable murder weapon—Jon from the garage and Mark from the carpenter's workshop. I think you had better tell all of this to the Police, *Mamm.*"

Sadie hesitated, would that be the right thing to do? If she told the Police, they might wade in too early and put the murderer on guard. It would be better to wait until there was further evidence.

One thing was certain; nothing was clear!

Katie worried about her mother. She was getting in too deep and if the murderer thought she was getting close, then who knew what might happen?

Sadie sat at the kitchen table, writing notes for herself, trying to make sense of the events of the last two days. Katie needed to get away, breath in some different air, but instead sat listlessly by the fire.

"Why don't you go and see Sarah, honey? I bet she needs a friend to talk to. I know the *schweschder's* weren't very close, but it will still be very traumatic for her. Poor girl, I bet she is feeling neglected in all of this."

The young girl shrugged. It would be better than doing nothing.

Sadie smiled; pleased to see her *dochder* put on her coat and venture outside the *haus*. It had been a trauma to them all and the sooner she could work out who the culprit was, the sooner life could start to get back to normal. Well, almost.

Sarah was pleased to see Katie. She hadn't been able to go out and could not bear the thought of people stopping her in the street and telling her how sorry they all were about Rebecca.

Katie was shocked to see how thin and pale Sarah was looking. Her eyes were red from crying and lined with dark circles from the lack of sleep. The least she could do was to try and comfort her for an hour or two.

Sarah was interested in how the case was going, how near the police were to catching her *schweschder's* killer. So with some relief, Katie unburdened herself of all her *mamm's* investigations to date and her concerns for her safety.

Back at the kitchen table, Sadie had written the names of the three possible culprits onto a clean sheet of paper.

Jon Stephenson, Mark Yoder, and Eli Lehman.

Sadie was convinced that the name of Rebecca's killer was staring right at her from the paper, but which one, and where was the final proof?

Jon Stephenson seemed to be a nice lad, but it was obvious that he had been Rebecca's boyfriend. He had admitted to Mark that he wanted to take things further with her but that she had backed off, unsure of herself and her faith. What if he had lost his temper? Maybe they were trying to make out in the woods, and she had changed her mind at the last minute? She knew what state young men could get into about sex. Maybe he was wound up, frustrated and didn't mean to do it. Perhaps it had just happened; before he knew what he was doing he had bashed her over the head with something heavy from the garage. No, that didn't work. If he was looking to make out with Rebecca, he wouldn't be carrying a heavy implement. Maybe he had killed her at the garage and dumped the body in the woods?

Then there was Mark Yoder. Mark was such a nice boy and she had known him since he was a baby. Surely, it couldn't be him? Yet, he had been besotted by Rebecca, had followed her around like a lost puppy. Rebecca had told Sadie all about him, how she had refused his invitations to supper, laughed at his constant attention. No man could put up with that for long, not even a gentle soul like Mark. Eventually his pride would have been hurt, he was a pious man, just like Eli, and maybe there were dark undertones beneath that smooth surface. Perhaps he had been following her that day into the woods, perhaps it was then that she told him about Jon, flaunted her affair with the *Englischer* to put him off?

And finally, there was Eli. Katie had already told her that Rebecca thought her *daed* followed her, kept tabs on where she was, what she was doing, and who she was with. What if Eli had seen her with Jon, what then? The shame and indignation would have almost killed him. She had witnessed his temper and had been afraid. But, could a *daed* really kill his own *dochder*? She had read about such things in the wider world, but it was a hard thing to comprehend.

Sadie sipped at her coffee, reading through her scribbles. Jealousy and hate were two of the most powerful emotions—

combined they were deadly.

The coffee slopped across the table as Sadie almost dropped her cup into the saucer.

"Katie!"

There was no time to lose. She had been so blind, why hadn't she seen it before, what if she was too late?

On the way across to the Lehman house, Sadie stopped off at Jacob King's barn. She needed to put in an urgent call to Dana Richards.

Reaching the Lehman door, Sadie knocked loudly to be let inside. Time was of the essence. As the door opened, Sadie pushed Martha aside and ran through the kitchen and up the stairs to the bedroom of Sarah, her heart beating wildly in panic.

Flinging back the bedroom door she was relieved to see the two girls chatting away together on the bed.

Martha had followed her upstairs, confused by the sudden urgency of her friend.

"What is it, Sadie; what's wrong?"

Looking back into the room, Sadie settled her gaze onto Sarah.

"I think I know who murdered your *dochder,* Martha. It was her own *schweschder!*"

The words did not make sense to Martha and she opened her mouth to speak but could not find the words. Perhaps Sadie was playing some kind of joke on them all, but it did not seem funny.

"It's obvious. She was jealous of Rebecca, jealous of her looks, and jealous of how her *daed* thought that she was perfect. Sarah was jealous that even the boy she loved only had eyes for

Rebecca. Jealousy had turned into hate. Isn't that right, Sarah?"

The room was silent and all eyes fell onto the young girl.

At first Sarah was silent, and then she began to shake as huge sobs of grief tugged at her body.

"I didn't mean to do it; it just happened."

"What happened in the woods, Sarah?"

Between the sobbing, Sarah started to confess. It was almost a relief to the poor girl.

"I was on my way home from working at the cafe. I didn't feel well and I had set off home early. Rebecca was walking back home with the shopping and we decided to take a short cut through the woods. She started teasing me about Mark Yoder, which wasn't fair. She knew that I was in love with him, but because of her I had no chance.

Suddenly, I saw red. I don't know why. All of those years of jealousy, of feeling second best. I just wanted her to feel the same hurt that I felt, and before I knew what I was doing, I had picked up a large rock and lashed out at her. I didn't mean to hit her on the head.

For a moment, I thought she was going to start laughing at me again. She had this strange expression on her face. And then I saw the blood, it started running down her face and into her eyes. She staggered back and fell to the floor. I panicked and ran home and left her. I didn't think she would die, I kept expecting her to walk back into the house. I never meant it... I wish to *Gott* that I could bring her back, I really do..."

Sarah's eyes were wild as she relived the experience.

Sadie felt a light tap on her shoulder. It was Dana Richards and she had come straight to the house. The detective inspector had heard every word of the confession and stepped forward to arrest the young girl.

Martha stood still, her hand clutching at the doorframe for support, not believing the scene that was playing out before her eyes. It was enough to lose one *dochder*, but this was almost too much to bear.

"What about Eli?"

Eli was out somewhere in the fields, trying to work though his grief. It was difficult to think what this would do to him.

"Pray for us, Sadie, please pray for us."

Martha followed her *dochder* out to the waiting police car. Sadie promised to sit and wait for Eli to return. She had no idea how she would break the news to him, the words she would use, what she would say. Eli would be a broken man.

Closing her eyes, she prayed to *Gott* to for guidance, remembering the lines of her favorite Psalm.

"The Lord is my shepherd; I shall not want. He maketh me to lie down in green pastures: he leadeth me beside the still waters. He restoreth my soul: he leadeth me in the paths of righteousness for his name's sake. Yea, though I walk through the valley of the shadow of death, I will fear no evil: for thou art with me; thy rod and thy staff they comfort me. Thou preparest a table before me in the presence of mine enemies: thou anointest my head with oil; my cup runneth over. Surely goodness and mercy shall follow me all the days of my life: and I will dwell in the house of the Lord for ever."

And she waited until the light began to fade, watching the sun sink wearily to the west and the shadows slowly gather across the room.

Made in the USA
Monee, IL
19 April 2023

31923009R00044